W9-CLI-733

For my three brothers—John, Douglas and Peter Stewart
—who know the magic of the Transcontinental
train whistle — H K - S

For Lexi and Ian, with thanks — P Z

Text copyright © 1997 Heather Kellerhals-Stewart
Illustrations copyright © 1997 Paul Zwolak

All rights reserved. No part of this book may be reproduced, stored in a retrieval system or transmitted
in any form or by any means, without the prior written permission of the publisher or, in the case of
photocopying or other reprographic copying, a licence from C A N C O P Y (Canadian Reprography
Collective), Toronto, Ontario.

Groundwood Books/Douglas & McIntyre
585 Bloor Street West
Toronto, Ontario M6G 1K5

Distributed in the U.S.A. by
Publishers Group West
4065 Hollis Street, Emeryville, CA 94608

The publisher gratefully acknowledges the assistance of the Canada Council
and the Ontario Arts Council.

Library of Congress data is available.

Canadian Cataloguing in Publication Data
Kellerhals, Stewart, Heather, 1937-
My brother's train
"A Groundwood book".
ISBN 0-88899-282-3
I. Zwolak, Paul. II. Title.
PS8571.E447M9 1997   jC813'.54   C96-932116-3
PZ7.K44My 1997

The artist wishes to thank the staff of Canadian Pacific Archives, Montreal,
for their gracious assistance.
The illustrations are painted in acrylic on canvas.
Design by Michael Solomon
Printed and bound in China by Everbest Printing Co. Ltd.

JP
K

My Brother's
TRAIN

BY

HEATHER
KELLERHALS-STEWART

PICTURES BY

PAUL ZWOLAK

OLD CHARLES TOWN LIBRARY, INC.
200 E. WASHINGTON ST.
CHARLES TOWN, WV 25414

A GROUNDWOOD BOOK

DOUGLAS & McINTYRE   VANCOUVER / TORONTO / BUFFALO

97004683

My brother has a very special train. It travels north and west for days and days. It's easy to go, but harder to come back. That's what my brother says.

Once, a long time ago, my brother took me on his train. While we waited in the station he asked me, "Do you have everything you need?"

"Yes, I've got all my stuff." And I showed him my toothbrush and socks and pants, wrapped up in a polka-dot scarf.

"That's good," he said. "Now tie it up, because here comes our train."

What I saw was a faraway cloud, coming closer and closer, until *ssss*... my brother and I were caught in the steam.

"All aboard for North Bay and points west," the conductor called.

I climbed the steps, holding my breath till we were through the steam.

"You take the window seat," my brother said. And so I did. My brother always spoils me.

Once, as the train was going underneath a bridge, I looked up and saw four faces staring down at me—three boys and a girl.

"Come on," my brother said "There's something I want to show you."

We walked through the train, holding tight where the coaches joined and swayed and the wheels squealed. At the very end we opened a door and stepped outside. It was almost dark.

"Do you see anything?" my brother asked.

"Only a slice of moon that's growing."

"Nothing else? Look back where the tracks turn into a V and the trees join hands."

"Is somebody running after our train?"

My brother smiled. "The trainman."

"Does he always follow the train?"

My brother nodded. "But not everyone knows he's there."

"Maybe he catches things that fall off the train or get left behind?" I asked.

"You could be right," he replied.

When we went back our seats were gone. The porter had changed them into berths—an upper and a lower.

"You take the one with the window," my brother said. And so I did. My brother always spoils me.

"Sometime during the night we'll be going over the height of land where the rivers flow to a different sea," my brother whispered from the upper berth.

Whoo, whooo… wailed the train whistle. *Clickety-clack* went the wheels. Over and over. Outside I couldn't see any lights, except the spark of an animal's eye.

Would I ever find my way home? But I thought of the trainman running behind and I soon fell asleep.

Next morning I looked out my window. My brother was right about it being harder to go back. I could get lost in the muskeg and the black-pointed trees.

"Did you hear the trainman during the night?" my brother asked. "Sometimes he sings as he runs."

"I fell asleep."

"That's good," my brother said.

Later, when the trees died out and the grass sprang up,
I saw a white horse running beside the tracks.

"A white horse brings you good luck," my brother said.
"Now find me a black one and double your luck."

For days and days we traveled…I guess. My brother stopped talking and opened a book. Finally he turned to me and said, "Who'll be the first to see the mountains?"

I looked and looked, but with my eye I could only see flatness. Was I ever glad when the train stopped to take on water.

"Fifteen-minute stop," the conductor called.

Before my brother could open his mouth I jumped off the train.

"Don't go too far," he called out the window.

"Only to the end of the platform," I promised. "No farther."

The platform was longer than I thought. At the very end I looked west to see what I could see. And there they were—clouds over the mountains.

"All aboard," the conductor called.

Steam rose from the engine, the whistle sounded. I ran down the platform. Faster and faster I flew, but the train did, too. My brother stood at the very back, holding out his hand. I could almost reach his fingers.

A voice sang in my ear, "Never fear, the trainman is here."

"Thanks," I heard my brother say, as he caught my hand.

Am I lucky my brother never gets mad at me.

Into the mountains the train climbed, until there was snow and rock all around.

"Where do we go now?" I wondered.

"Into the spiraling tunnels," my brother said. "Into the sounding darkness."

My brother was right. I had to cover my ears and hold my breath. What would the trainman do in the noise and soot—close his eyes and sneeze?

Just when I was thinking we'd never see light again, the train burst into sunshine. A river sparkled beside the tracks.

"The river that flows to the sea," my brother said.

"I bet I could float all the way down it."

"You probably could," he agreed.

I grew sleepier and sleepier as the train ran on.

"Can you smell the ocean?" my brother asked.

"Something seaweedy and sandy," I murmured. "Maybe a starfish high and dry..."

"Last stop," the conductor called. "Arriving in ten minutes' time."

"End of the line," my brother said.

I was too sleepy to care. My brother had to take my hand as we climbed off the train.

An old lady who was waiting for us there squeezed me in a hug.

"Say how-do-you-do to your great-aunt Muriel," my brother said.

And so I did.

Great-aunt Muriel's cottage smelled of mothballs, cedar trees and salt and sand. Her cookies did, too. But what I liked best was the rocky point with the lighthouse that called through the fog. Over and over.

Finally one day I told my brother. "I've had enough cookies and I'm tired of squishing sand in my shoes. How much longer are we staying?"

"Time's almost up," my brother told me. "I heard a train whistle from far away. Come on," he said, grabbing my hand. "We'd better hurry. It's easy to go, but harder to come back…"

And we ran and we ran to catch the train.

"You're just in time," the trainman sang. "I've saved you a spot in the dining car. It's chicken à la king with peas, followed by a dessert spectacular."

Yes, that's how it was. But you can ask my brother if you like.

JP   97004683
Kellerhals-Stewart, Heather
My brother's train

OLD CHARLES TOWN LIBRARY
CHARLES TOWN, WV 25414

DEMCO